Clutch Your Pearls, Girls

A Second Collection of #CowBios

ISBN: 979-8-218-96749-9

Any references to historical events, real people, or real places are used fictitiously. Names, characters, and places are products of the author's imagination.

Front cover image by Rachel Gabel

Front cover and book design by Liz Banman Munsterteiger

Independently published in the United States of America

First printing edition 2024

Rachel Gabel

rachelgabelco@gmail.com

www.rachelgabel.com

This is a rare sighting of me and three of my favorite humans in the same zip code.

We have a group message that would scare mere mortals and it has to replace actual time together.

We dole out recipes, advice, prayers, prayer requests, grammatical advice, news, questions, answers, and keep up a steady stream of communication using song lyrics, memes, and words.

They are the smartest, most faithful, and fiercest women I know.

They're excellent spellers. They cheer loudly for their friends.

They understand the Gospel of Carrie's Scotcheroos and will preach it when snacks are in order.

They hoard fancy pens. They look forward to new planner season.

They understand things that just don't bear the weight of words.

Thanks, pals.

For my mama

She's the reason I'm smart and funny.

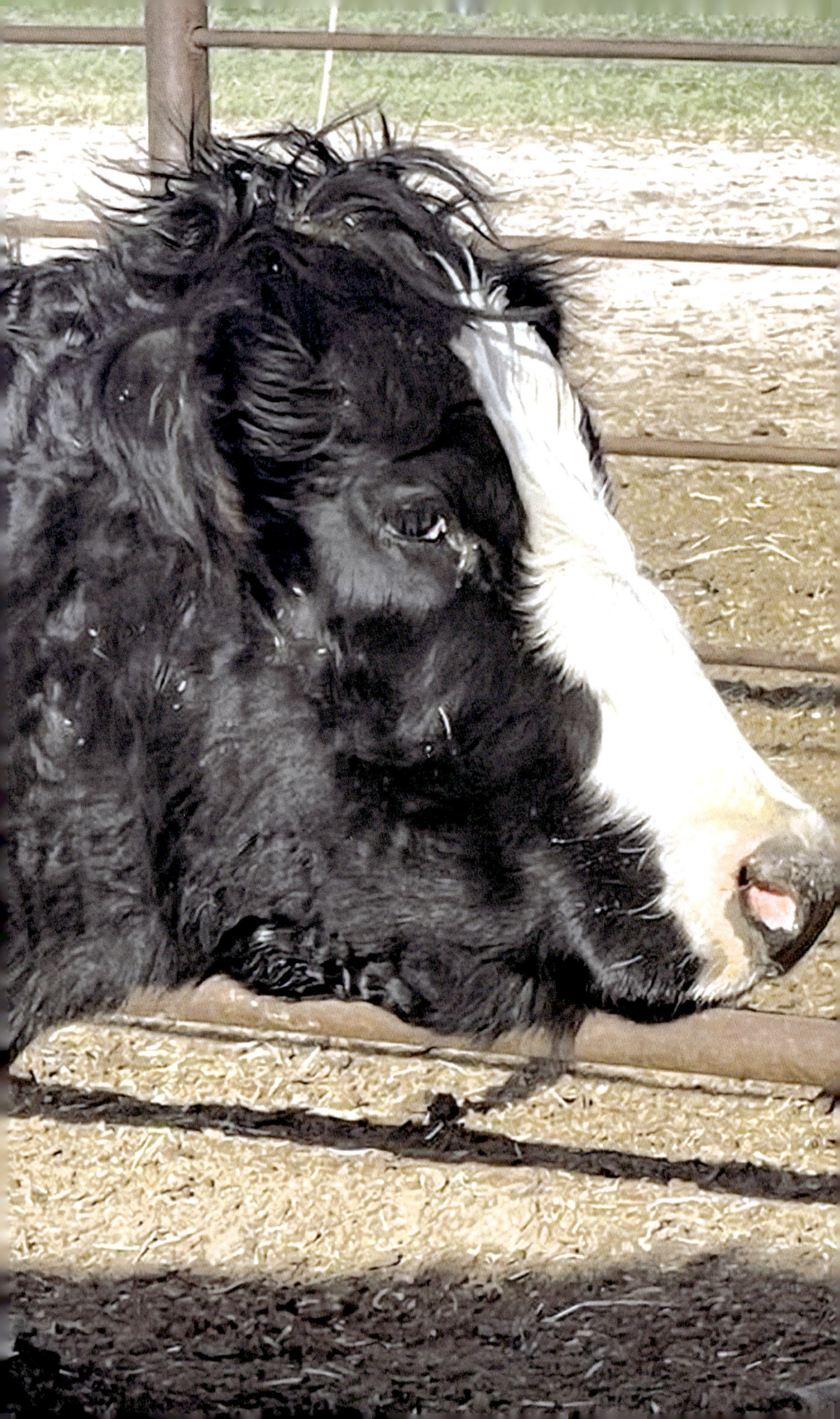

THIS IS *Meredith*

The kids are back to school and absolutely exhausted, coughing during the night, and have no concept of bedtime. Rather than creating a serene kitchen made for organization, routines, and systems, she is in full-blown garden harvest mode. Boxes of jars and freezer bags are stacked in corners and every flat surface has boxes of cucumbers, squash, tomatoes, jalapeños, and more cucumbers.

If she's spicy, it's only because she stayed up until midnight cutting, cleaning, and bagging roasted green chiles. Her hands and right eyeball are still *on fire*.

She has made dill pickles, bread-and-butter pickles, fermented pickles, and cinnamon pickles.

She stealthily moved away from the cool moms the other day after school when one said she had a sudden craving for dill pickles, knowing vinegar is seeping from her pores. She's sure that in another month, the canning and freezing will be done and her kitchen will be back to perfect order.

Of course, she's been known to dream. Relish the harvest, gals.

THIS IS

BINGO! *She has BINGO!*

They came home from state fair last night but not before she filled out her BINGO card.

She had:

B: a feral fair orphan with ice cream on his face and his parents unaware of his location;

I: body-suit wearing fairgoers with body suits either flesh-colored spandex or hand crocheted and unlined;

N: a fair mom with a slow cooker, three stocked coolers, and kids begging for a chunk of cheese on a stick breaded and deep fried and sold for $20;

G: fairgoers with the trifecta- a Playboy bunny tattoo, a scrap of synthetic fabric covering some body parts, and a stuffed animal backpack;

O: a last year exhibitor's mom loading up for the last time and wondering what she's going to do with herself next summer.

BINGO indeed.

DABEL
0117

ROSE

She gave in and took her children to the state fair carnival, despite her disdain for crowds and germs. They went on a few rides and then found the giant slide. Perhaps it was a lapse in judgment—or temporary insanity—but she agreed to join them.

The little guys went down the slide, over the gentle bumps, and to the bottom. Then it was her turn. She sat down on the Wrangler patch-sized burlap scrap and eased into the leisurely trip. Her kids watched and cheered. She waved.

That was her first mistake.

A curve took her by surprise and tipped her back like a winter Olympian minus the spandex and snow. Her shirt blew up, and her arms were sealed down by the speed she was building. She hit the next two bumps at blinding speed and hurtled further down the slide like a chubby, adrenalin-loving penguin.

She thought she may be breaking existing land speed records when she hit the last section of slide. She shot into the mats meant to break her landing like a bowling ball rolled by a Bowl-a-Rama regular. She had attracted the attention of onlookers and to her horror, several of them came to assist her removal of her body from the cracks in the mat.

She was secretly relieved, especially when one found her shoe. The upside is knowing—even now—that she's downright aerodynamic. *Whee!*

PHOTO BY JACKIE MARIE

THIS IS

She spent Saturday at the State Fair. She's seen *some things*. She's seen more thighs and breasts than a KFC fry cook and has cataloged 163 ways to wear various items that aren't shirts as shirts.

Don't even get her started on the women's outfits.

It's hot enough to encourage people to do shady things in front of porta coolers—but she absolutely understands that. It's the show barn equivalent to a Klondike bar, and she knows what she would do to cool off.

She has all the exhibitor paperwork, fitting supplies, buckets, and kids basically accounted for, and she has a spot near a fan and the cooler. She can also report only two misspelled tattoos.

No regerts, girls. No regerts.

PHOTO BY AMANDA LAURIDSON

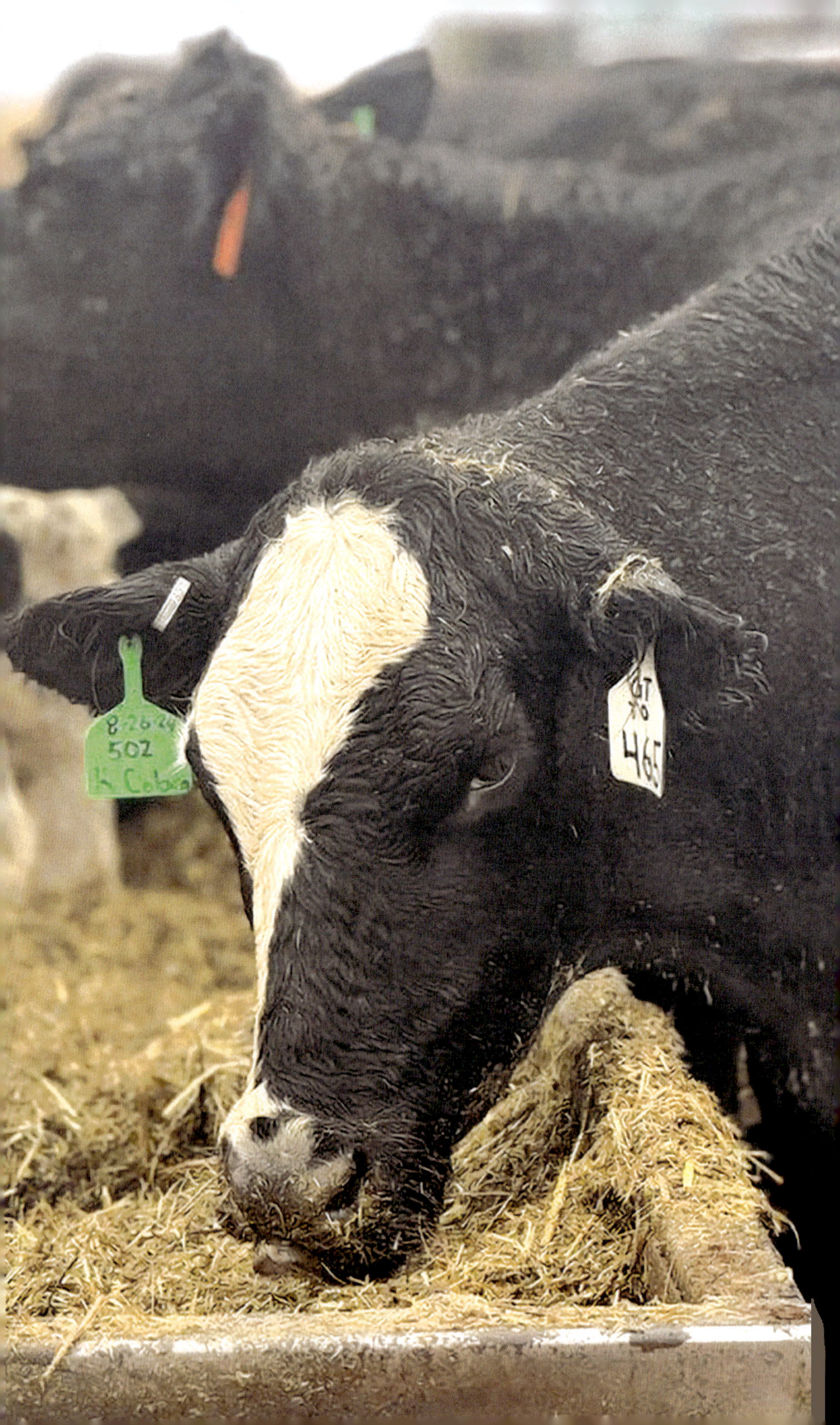
8-26-24
502
465

THIS IS *Maria*

She didn't drink coffee until after she turned 40. That gas station white chocolate caramel cappuccino is a gateway drug. Now it's iced and Keurig, and even her blended chai latte is dirty.

But something's gotta give, because once the caffeine wears off so does her will to function, parent cheerfully, and not commit felonies in Walmart. She's trying to decide whether to go cold turkey and if her morning peach mango V-8 Energy is *really* considered caffeine.

She's not sure caffeine is really the problem. Maybe functioning is stupid, parenting isn't supposed to be cheerful and sometimes felonies just need to be committed in Walmart. But she'll try it. Immediately.

Well, she looked at her calendar and this isn't a good week. She checked in with her hormones and next week doesn't look good either.

She's going to quit the caffeine. She will, she tells herself as she adds Keurig, Folgers, and V-8 Energy to her Walmart shopping list.

THANK YOU, MARIA TIBBETTS

THIS IS *Mrs. A*

She and her kids have returned to school—her in the 29th grade and the littles in 1st and 6th. Adrenaline and iced coffee carried her through the first week and a half, but she has since hit a wall. A new strain of sinus infection is making them all feel like they're breathing through lukewarm gelatin, and they're coughing like they've been smoking since cigarette ads were a thing.

She drew the three ornery boys in her classroom, though she does currently have the upper hand—and their mothers on speed dial. Her feet feel like she has jogged across a desert barefoot, and she never even considered wearing anything other than practical shoes with ample arch support and cushion. The pants that fit her in May *almost* fit her again after a summer of margs.

Thank goodness it's Thursday, because she doesn't have three more days in her. *Pass the caffeine and lunch on a tray, girls. Let's do this.*

PHOTO BY TRACY MOORE

THIS IS *Nancy*

She is ready for her weather to be a little more *sweater*, and a little less *sweaty*. You can keep your swamp-sock, sunburned, soggy summer weather with its frizzy hair and exasperating chub rub.

There has to be something grand between makeup melting hellfire and subzero horizontal snow. Right? *Surely*. She's ready to grill burgers outside in a sweatshirt and shorts like the 65-degree diva she pretends to be.

Bring on the weather that allows for car chapsticks to survive the day. She's here for it—though you can keep your fancy pumpkin spiced coffees. She will continue to run on iced coffee and salted rims, just without the sweat.

PHOTO BY SARAH LANIK-FRAIN

THIS IS *Ramona*

There are a few conversations with her daughter that she wasn't ready for and she marked one off the list last night. The first step, obviously, was a quick text conversation with The Besties. Call it crowd-sourcing, call it a pep talk...that's just how they roll.

A few minutes later, Ramona was trying to impress upon the girl child the importance of long, slow razor strokes. She assured her that she wouldn't grow werewolf hair if she skipped a day and doubled down on the keys to kneecap safety.

Then, when the homemade pizzas were on the table and Ramona had a chance to drink, a young woman walked out of her room grinning. *Dear Lord,* there's nothing easy about raising kids. Light a candle and pass the bandaids, girls. Things just got real.

PHOTO BY TRACY MOORE

THIS IS *Blaykeleigh*

She will be a sophomore in college in a couple weeks. This is her casual fair look—why do you ask? She has no idea why old ladies with dull, for-or-five-letter names always stare at her funny when she spells her name, or exactly what they mean when they look at her and say, "Just wait 20 years, dear."

Well, she for one will *not* have random gray hairs on her chin, nor will she volunteer at the fair concession stand, dressed in a stained graphic tee she was seen wearing the day before, criticizing teenagers in crop tops. She won't tote off-brand water containers, allow her eyebrows to grow wild, have kids who act like lunatics in public, or wear shoes based on comfort instead of style. She has no concept of what small children can do to a woman's purse, car, or midsection.

She is naturally toned, tanned for summer, and a smart go-getter of a young lady with a trail of local boys tripping over themselves in her wake. But as those dull, older gals say, just you wait, sweetheart. It's a wild ride from where you are to where they are. But, most will tell you it's more than worth it. Sticky purse, lunatic kids, gray chin hairs, and all.

THANK YOU, HEATHER MAUDE

She woke up this morning without a kink in her neck, the sky was the perfect blue, and the dogs didn't wake her up once in the night. But when the cat peeked out of the bathtub her perfect morning flattened a little. The twitchy calico feline stared at the shower curtain in the corner. Pam didn't want to know, but she didn't want to wonder. She moved the curtain.

The mouse scurried to hide behind a shampoo bottle. The cat twitched, but stayed calm.

Judging by the state of the bathtub this game had gone on for some time and the mouse was quite literally scared shitless. Pam groaned at the thought of cleaning it up. She established that there was no escape route for the mouse. The calico empress must have imported the hapless gladiator mouse for her own entertainment, to be disposed of at her leisure. The clever cat had managed to find a waist-friendly solution to the problem of "I'm not hungry, but I'm bored."

Pam shut the bathroom door and hoped the cat got hungry.

Two hours later she checked the carnage. There was just a twitchy cat and an even more scared shitless mouse. Pam decided to take matters into her own hands—partly because she didn't want the cat to keep torturing the mouse, partly because she didn't want to risk it escaping.

She suspected this was the mouse responsible for shredding the new rolls of toilet paper in the drawer and leaving a decidedly negative personal message on her bra in the laundry one night. Pam fetched a board and with a few swift smacks dispatched the creature and hauled his carcass outside, then returned to clean up the bathtub.

The cat had already left the bathtub for other diversions, probably wondering what she was going to have for lunch now. Pam may not be as badass as her mom, who killed a pencil-sized rattlesnake on the basement floor with a croquet mallet, but she feels like she's getting a little closer.

THANKS, MARIA TIBBETTS. PHOTO BY LOY COTTEN

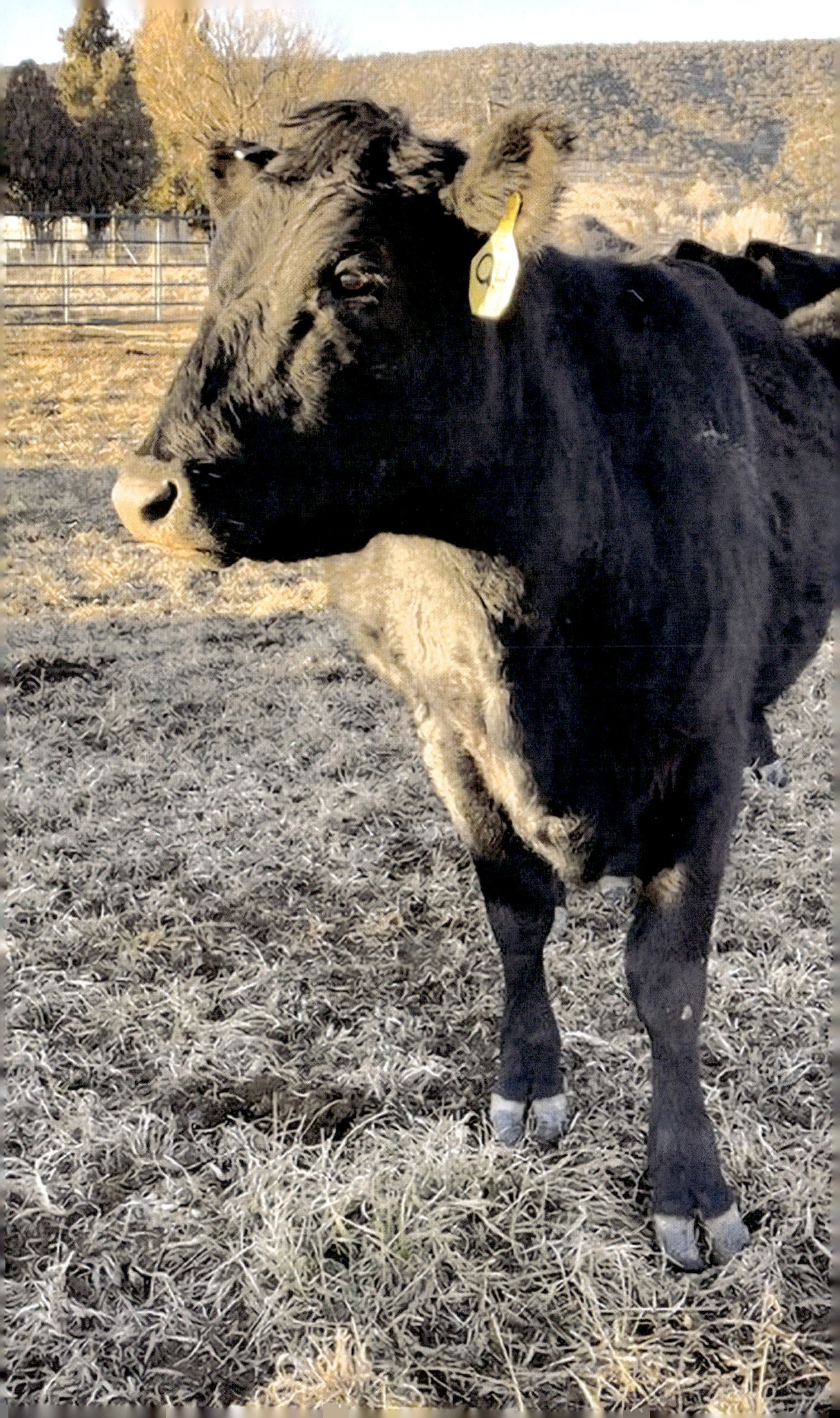

112

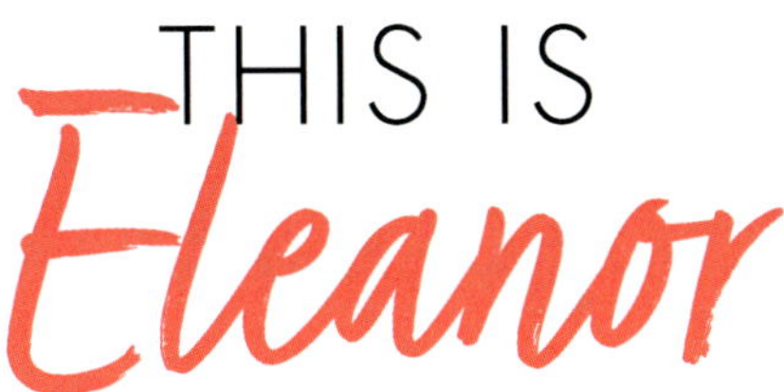

She has strong opinions on carrot cake, diet pop, and tacos. She's a staunch Conservative and appreciates the recipes of the Methodist and Catholic Churches in town. She has thoughts on mayonnaise, deli meats, and Baptism.

She drives domestic made cars and the larger the better, especially the trunk. Better to transport the mayo-based and complicated gelatin salads. She hasn't used a turn signal in years and when pulled over once, explained to the young man that she's been turning on that very street since he was a mere twinkle in his daddy's eye and everyone knows it.

She believes in pearls, manners, and that the internet is what's wrong with this country. If you need her, consult the Baptist Church bulletin. It's practically her social calendar.

Now, get busy, young lady. And sit up straight.

PHOTO BY TRACY MOORE

THIS IS *Fern*

She's starting another year of teaching this week. The bulletin boards are ready for artwork created by sticky hands, the desks are neatly labeled, and the cubbies are lined up and awaiting new crayons and folders, and disinfecting wipes. *Lots* of disinfecting wipes.

She teaches in a small town, so she knows many of the faces that will be at her classroom door in the morning. She's also the praying kind:

> "Lord, watch over the teachers and the kids as parents shine their little faces and send them to school. Help them all be brave, whether they're nervous about a new school, a new routine, or about finding what they're supposed to do with a quiet house during these weekdays.
>
> Help the teachers see each child and their potential, as well as their desire to succeed and earn their praise. Help the kids be kind to one another, and to seek out and include the kids who are doing their best to look brave.
>
> Bless the hands who are welcoming them back, preparing their meals, and doling out high fives like they're throwing candy at a parade. Help the parents be strong, supportive, and willing to pay for the teacher behind them in line at the liquor store—all while pretending not to see them. *Amen.*"

PHOTO BY SAMANTHA CUNNINGHAM

She's at the Hobby Lobby nearing holiday decor overwhelm and looking for a cute sign for her kitchen.

Gather? No.

Choose happiness? Nope, she'll have anxiety with a side of overwhelm, thanks.

Follow me to paradise? She snort laughed to herself and thought someone could follow her to the gas pumps, school, ball fields, The Walmart, and down the road paved with good intentions. Probably not paradise though.

Live, Laugh, Love? Eye roll.

Welcome to our farmhouse? Sure. Move the tractor part off the kitchen table and have a seat. I promise not to put milk replacer or LA-200 in your coffee if you promise not to look at the floor under my table.

She settled on walking aimlessly around the store and resisting the urge to purchase paper planners in various sizes with good pens. Light a candle for her, girls.

PHOTO BY SUE LINK

THIS IS Jolene

She's planning a birthday party for her daughter. She requested a purple themed party. Guess which color The Walmart didn't have.

She dug a bit and hit the jackpot. She filled her cart like it was Black Friday and the Cabbage Patch Kid-seeking hoardes were bearing down on her. She had Dolly Parton plates, a silver Dolly Parton table cover, *Ya'll Need Dolly* napkins, *What Would Dolly Do* plates, and all the sparkly Dolly Parton paraphernalia.

Her daughter is thrilled. Her daughter was raised right.

She waited all day for her husband to ask when the party starts. Six, she told him.

Then she stuck her head around the corner and asked if he knew why.

Then she broke into song. "*Workin' 9 to 5...*"

He may have reconsidered his life decisions but she chuckled to herself the rest of the night.

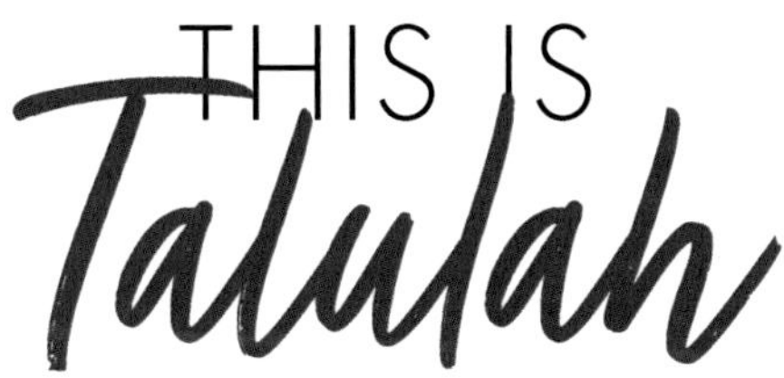

She listened patiently to the news report touting ecosystem balance and coexistence. She listened to the guy with lots of letters behind his name say the beasts are *"totally chill"* and harmless.

She calmly turned the news off, shut the lights off, and prepared for battle.

The house was dark save for a single lightbulb burning over the kitchen sink. She ran hot water into the sink and mixed the dish soap until it was bubbling and reaching toward the lightbulb.

In the morning, she tallied the corpse count and threw the dirty beasts outside in a wave of dirty water.

The battle has begun. She hasn't yet won the war, but she's ready for combat.

Friggin moths.

THIS IS *Heather*

Her garden grows a bit larger each year, but this year, it is a bit daunting even to her. Obviously, she needs to purchase seeds. Since December, she has been adding to her significant stockpile.

It began as a handful of packets with a rubber band around them. Then it moved to a gallon baggie, then a coffee can, and now it's in a Rubbermaid tub.

She has been ordering as she's falling asleep at night, too, which has resulted in mail deliveries she may have forgotten about. She has 10 varieties of pumpkins, 20 flavors of zinnias, and she's lost count of the sunflower varieties she has stashed in the tub.

After planting for two days, a package arrived in the mail. She opened it and dealt the packs into the tub like an old casino scene with $100 bills.

Don't remind her that she's going to have to weed this beast.

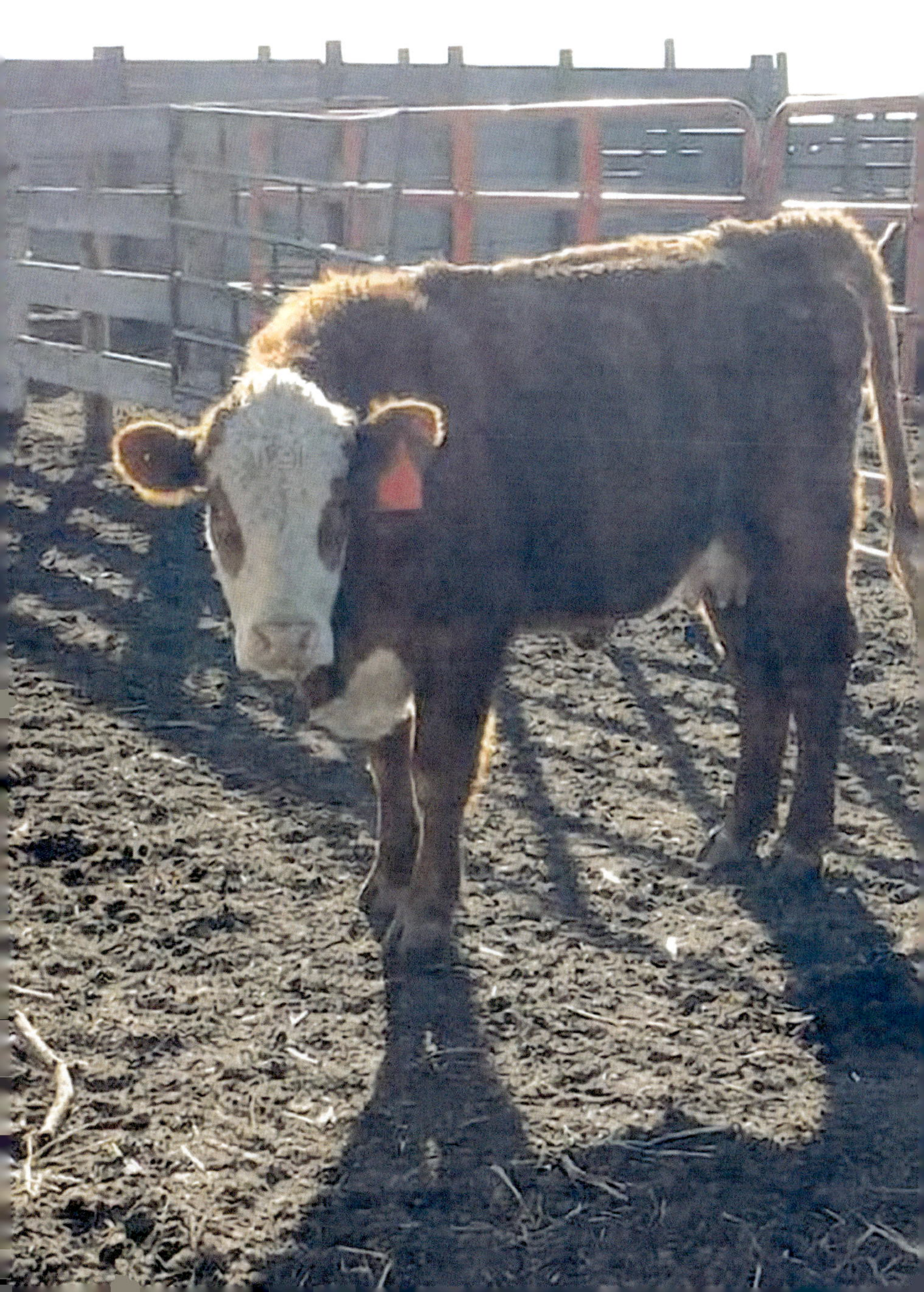

401
4269

THIS IS *Madalyn*

She has been preparing for Memorial Day with a grateful heart and a green thumb.

Before her grandfather was an old man who taught little girls to eat cantaloupe with salt on the porch before the day became hot, he saw the Pacific Theater and held the hand of his brother as he died. She carefully decorated both markers, especially the one marking the life of a young man who would be forever 19.

Red geraniums were carefully curated for her grandmother's grave. She had rocked on another porch, surrounded by red geraniums, and smoked and watched Madalyn try to hula hoop. She also had red geraniums for her grandmother's youngest brother, lost to the war on the day before victory was declared.

Madalyn, once satisfied with her arrangements, walked to a part of the cemetery that wasn't crowded with families, where the graves were dark with age. On her hands and knees, she tidied and weeded. She cut back the plants placed long ago by families that missed them. Young men in uniform, babies, young mothers, young men who lived—and died—in hard times

While not buried with military honors, Madalyn made sure each was remembered. She walked back through the portion of the cemetery filled with white crosses and whispered her thanks before driving slowly away.

THIS IS *Earlene*

Don't talk to her. She's not in the mood for small talk. She's recovering from not one but *two* traumatic events in her life. She's reeling. *Pray for her.* She's concentrating on self-care and nutrition until she's strong enough to return to normal. She's weak, nauseated, and gets dizzy and shaky when she thinks back to that day.

She'll tell you, but only because her friend suggested she talk it out.

It was late in the evening, and she had been deep in the drama for days. She couldn't escape it, day or night. She just kept listening to the voices and being led deeper. And then it was over. She looked around, expecting someone to tease her or console her, but she was alone. The voices had fallen silent. *The audiobook was over.*

When she finally gathered the strength to begin another, the Kansas accents of ranch men sounded like whiny line dancers in Alabama. She couldn't return. *Wouldn't return.* And now, her world is silent and she'll never know how the story ends.

Damn you, Audible.

254

THIS IS

She's getting a bit older than she cares to admit. She saw herself today in a store window and spun around, thinking her mom had joined her. Nope. The resemblance is uncanny.

She knows the importance of annual once-overs, and today is the day. She told the dermatologist she was seeing more and more spots on her face and hands these days.

My mom, she said, *used to call these liver spots.* She cringed at her own mention of liver, reminding her of liver and onions served up at the old folks home. She shuddered.

She looked at her hands and legs, covered in what may have once been coveted freckles, but are now old looking. Liver spots. *Ugh.*

The dermatologist looked at her. *They're still called liver spots, Violet.*

She'll be crying in her car with a diet cherry limeade if you need her geriatric self.

THIS IS *Wilhelmina*

She believes in standing out in a crowd. She believes accessories make the woman, and she has signature pieces that she wears without fail. You can call her Zsa Zsa Gabor—that's the vibe she's going for.

Heck. It's hard not to stand out when you're a statuesque redhead.

The one regret is that night when she and her bestie thought it a good idea to walk into the tattoo parlor. Despite years of jokes about *"better a W than an L"* and stares from strangers and small kids, it—and an ex-husband—remain mistakes that are tough to shake.

So, she chooses to let her ink remind her of the young woman who jumped on the back of a Harley with a ruggedly handsome, leather-clad man and let the wind blow her hair. She chooses to be reminded of the young woman who had smooth thighs and big hair.

Some decisions are forever, and she's made better ones, but *dang*, she had a good time making the bad ones.

PHOTO BY GINNY HARRINGTON

THIS IS Emmy

Her mother has told her a number of things. In fact, she has talked herself blue in the face. She has given Emmy all of her best advice: wear sunscreen, you only get one set of adult teeth so take care of them, sensible shoes matter, say please, and wear your seatbelt.

There are a number of higher-level nuggets that her mother has added over the years. Don't argue with people online, lipstick matters, moisturize, enunciate, write neatly, and don't eat with the abandon of a wild hog in public.

Emmy has heard that she should read daily, use prayer as a first response rather than a last resort, and be kind to people, especially when you don't want to be kind. Emmy does her best, though today is a reminder from her to you that perhaps the best advice is *not to stick your nose where it doesn't belong.*

Happy Monday, Emmy.

THIS IS *Laura*

Thank you for noticing! She *did* cut bangs!

She was just ready to update her look and do a little something to look younger. She's no spring chicken, you know. The influencer video she watched said bangs are totally in style, especially with the monochrome hair look. She just did exactly what the YouTube video said to do, and they came out *just perfect.*

She's going to try waxing next!

She ran into the grocery store this morning. About halfway through the pasta aisle, she realized she knew the song playing over the speaker. Then she realized it was the same song she used to listen to while getting ready—at midnight—to go to the bar.

The same song she used to listen to while at the bar jumping and bouncing with no fear of gravity or pee, and the same song that made her think of Zima and Tommy Girl perfume.

Then, while she was waiting for school pickup, one of the moms mentioned her kids had been watching a movie that came out the same year she was born. Olivia is no mathlete, but realized that other mom was born the same year she was tight-rolling her jeans and roller skating.

Awesome. Pass the denture cream, girls.

PHOTO BY JANIE VANWINKLE

THIS IS *Thelma*

She requests that the record accurately reflect her formal motion that the month of May back up before she is forced to hit it right in the actual nose.

May has been one birthday, bridal shower, wedding, first communion, Mother's Day, field trip, field day, state test, baccalaureate, confirmation, 4-H meeting, deadline, banquet, livestock judging contest, jackpot, plant sale, graduation, dress up day, luncheon, funeral, staff meeting, and branding after a freaking other.

She isn't sure whose great idea it was to squeeze three Decembers into one month, make the pollen plentiful, and the emotions high, but she isn't impressed. She objects, in fact.

If you need her, she'll be sitting in her car in the driveway, staring into space and trying to gather the intestinal fortitude to get out of said vehicle.

Light a candle for her, girls.

980

502
GT
TO
465

THIS IS *Laurie*

Her friend is oily. Not in a "somebody's spoiled oil patch wife" bumper sticker way, but in an *essential oils* way.

She offhandedly mentioned an earache once and her friend was like a guy selling Rolex watches from inside his suit coat on a NYC corner. She whipped oregano out of somewhere and treated the earache. Laurie won't confirm or deny its effectiveness.

Once she mentioned feeling nervous and her friend whipped out lavender essential oil faster than Pony Boy pulling out a switchblade.

Today, she mentioned feeling on edge and said she couldn't remember what someone recommended to quiet her mind and slow her racing thoughts. Her friend asked if it had perhaps been *Clary Sage.* No. *Bergamot?* No. *Ylang ylang?* Nope. *Citrus Reticulata?* No...

Then she told her friend she remembered what it was called.

Marjoram?

No.

Chloroform. That's what it was.

Her friend fainted.

This is the most flattering photo in existence of poor Hilda. This is the photo her family chose to share on social to wish her a happy Mother's Day.

She doesn't care, though. It's a dang sight better than her drivers license photo. It's not a mug shot. It's also not a glamour shot.

She has a headshot for work but, as she's told her family, if she ever goes missing,it's this photo—not the headshot or driver's license photo—that ought to be shared on the news.

If the drivers license photo is shared, people will be too afraid to approach her a la the *"put your chin down and don't smile"* look courtesy of the DMV. If her headshot is shared, they'll be looking for someone less fluffy, less gray, and more pleasant looking.

This. *This* is the photo to share if there's anyone ambitious enough to kidnap her.

That is, obviously, why she eats ice cream. Harder to kidnap.

Carry on.

9954

She has been using her Oil of Olay and is a big fan of the makeup tutorials on The Facebook. Contouring is no sweat, skincare is second nature, but these dang glasses hide her lashes.

She has, however, mastered the smoky eye. Because the magazines of her youth suggested she would need looks to go from day to night, she can go from cash register to bowling alley and look good going.

You just can't beat the smoldering natural look, and baby, she's owning it.

Beauty is on the inside, but good mascara never hurt a dang thing.

PHOTO BY NICOLE WANDREY

THIS IS Greta

She passed the talkinest woman in America on her first trip down the grocery aisle. She finally shook loose, grabbed a few items, and turned the corner. She was grabbing salsa and chicken broth and canned corn and diced tomatoes.

She rounded the corner and saw her pal. She considered skipping an aisle but she knew, beyond a doubt, that if she veered from her routine, she would be turned around the rest of the trip. She took a deep breath and only stood and nodded as her pal talked for 15 minutes.

She was going to miss school pick-up if she didn't hustle. Even though it was a small town, there was still four aisles. She grabbed some bubbly water, a bag of tater tots, and ice cream and hit the road.

She wasn't even in the car yet when the gal started texting her.

Settle down, bestie. Settle down.

She had a fleeting moment this week when she forgot who she was and she allowed herself to feel less than. Then she called on her besties. They reminded her that she is not only a daughter of the King, but is one bad bitch.

She is good at more things than she's bad at, can carry eight bags of groceries at once, makes a mean white gravy, drinks ample amounts of water, knows her tire size by heart, mostly remembers to text people back, can back a trailer while men are watching, and makes a carrot cake that'll make you want to slap yo mama.

Straighten your crown, gal.

By the time the fires were put out at her remote job and diapers were changed, she knew she was running late.

She put the pickup in reverse and took a deep breath. Trailers—specifically those in need of hooking up—can smell fear. Or rather, they can smell when Mom is behind schedule.

All preparations were made: a pacifier was placed in baby's mouth to reduce screaming during the crucial period, dry cleaning hangers were moved to the side, trailer jacked up to desired height, and two carefully chosen pieces of gravel were placed one foot apart on the tailgate to give her a visual buffer.

She stood on tiptoes in the driver's seat to see said markers, then the dirty ranch truck slowly crept back. *No sudden moves.* Steady. Steady.

Not being quite tall enough to see the ball, she backed up a reasonable distance and got out to eyeball. She shut one eye for accuracy.

Backed up six more inches.

Got out.

Backed one more inch.

Got out.

Forward a half inch. *Perfect.*

Annie began jacking the trailer down. The hitch didn't land quite right, but she hoped she could make it work. Getting back in the pickup, she pulled the age-old trick of driving forward a few inches and slamming on the brakes.

BANG. The trailer slid into place and she was good to go. A quick job of hooking up lights and safety chains and dropping the pin and she was road ready. Only ten minutes late.

Now to catch that snaky gray mare. She can smell fear, too.

THANK YOU, KAYCEE MONNENS CORTNER

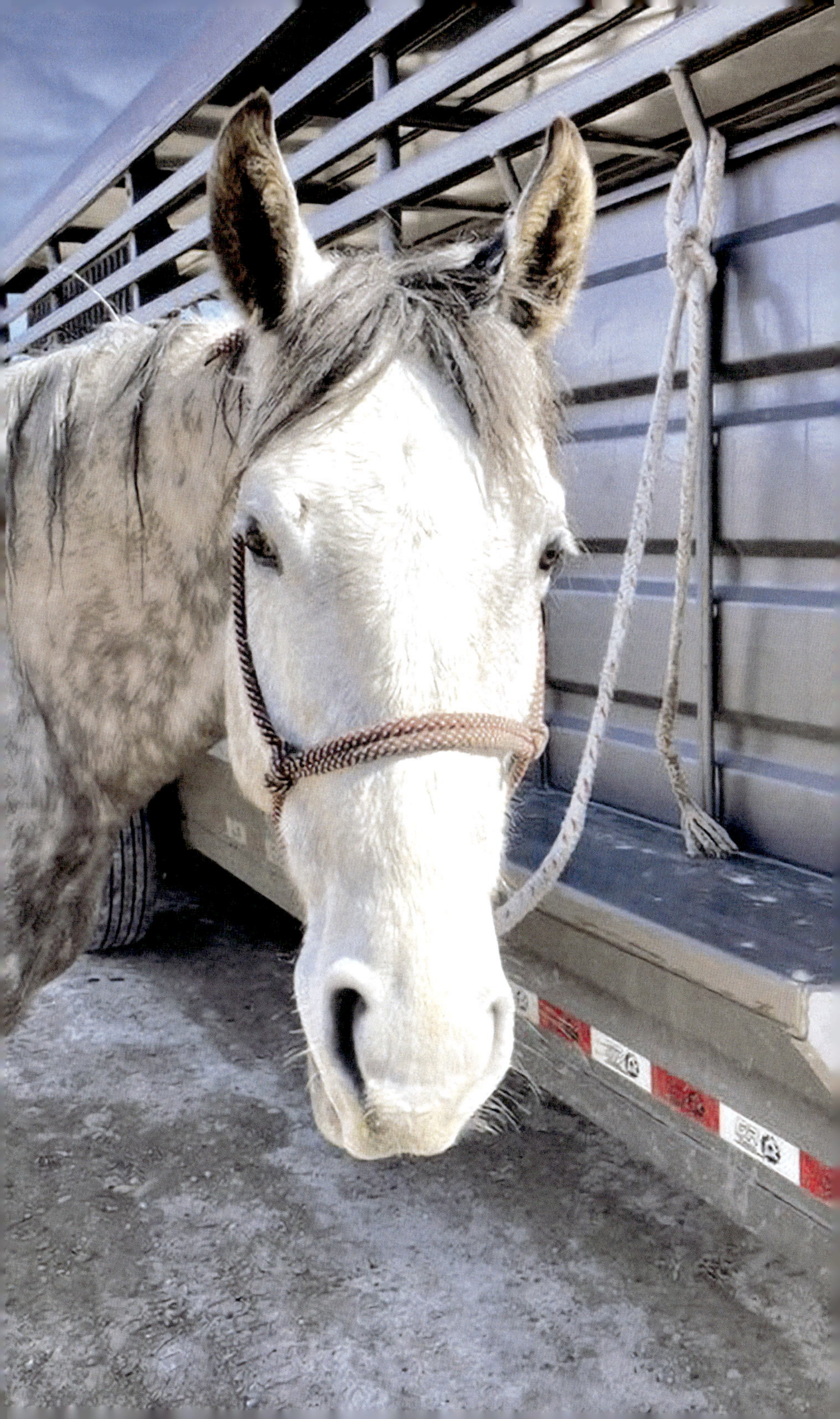

THIS IS *Clementine*

She is so freaking far behind that she has decided to just start over. Once she did, for a few glorious moments, she was caught up and awash with tranquility and peacefulness. She could string more than three monosyllabic words together to form a complete thought. She could even look people in the eye and she refrained from talking incessantly about anything that might make eavesdroppers clutch their proverbial pearls.

Annnnnnnnd, the moment has passed.

She is solidly back on shaky ground with a to-do list that makes the Harry Potter series books look like light reading. She doesn't know what day it is. She doesn't know the coordinates of the nearest toll road, the number in her graduating class, or the mileage from Hays, Kansas, to Pawhuska, Oklahoma. She does, however, know that reading and writing cursive is a life skill and that carrot cake is basically a salad.

Someday she will tackle the 10,817 unread emails, 78 texts, and 30,198 photos on her phone and the list of no fewer than 70 voicemails.

Today, though, isn't that day, kids.

She's tired of the wind. Not just tired like she ate one too many salads for lunch, but the kind of tired that boils and churns in her chest and her darkened little soul.

If the wind were a woman, she's certain she would jump her in the bathroom and walk out like a '90s mob wife. If wind were a woman, she would be a crummy bowler who insists, between sips of cheap wine, that it's unusual for her to be less than legendary.

If wind were a woman, she would be the mom in the school drop-off line who must be making her kid an omelet in that minivan based on how long the line has been stacking up behind her. She would be hard to escape from at The Walmart and would suggest weight loss hacks and potions in a one-sided conversation.

What a gem, she would be. Run along.

THIS IS *Delilah & Dawna*

They're driving together and spot a road sign: *Limon - 10 miles.*

Delilah, who is from a small town, says they'll stop in Limon. Dawna, who poo-poos rural America, says, *"Did you just say Limon? You're pronouncing it wrong. It's Limon."*

They go back and forth for ten miles until Delilah finally decides they'll stop at the first place they see and ask exactly how Limon is pronounced. Fine.

The two park, walk inside, and approach the gal at the counter.

"Would you please tell this dumb country girl, very clearly and slowly, just where we are?" Dawna smiles.

The gal looks from Delilah to Dawna, then leans across the counter to be eyeball-to-eyeball with the pair.

"L-o-a-f n J-u-g," she says.

Dawna fainted.

THIS IS

Her kids were telling her about attending the play *Cinderella*. Someone said, "*Cinderella dressed in yellow...*" Rosie wasted no time in picking up where they left off with the enthusiasm that surprised even her.

"Come sit next to me, you fine fellow!"
You run over there without a second to lose
And what comes next? hey, bust a move!
If you want it, you got it
If you want it, baby, you got it,
If you want it, you got it
If you want it, baby, you got it...

It was silent until finally, the noise of her daughter rolling her eyes could be heard around the room. Her husband was questioning his life decisions.

Don't just stand there, Rosie, bust a move.

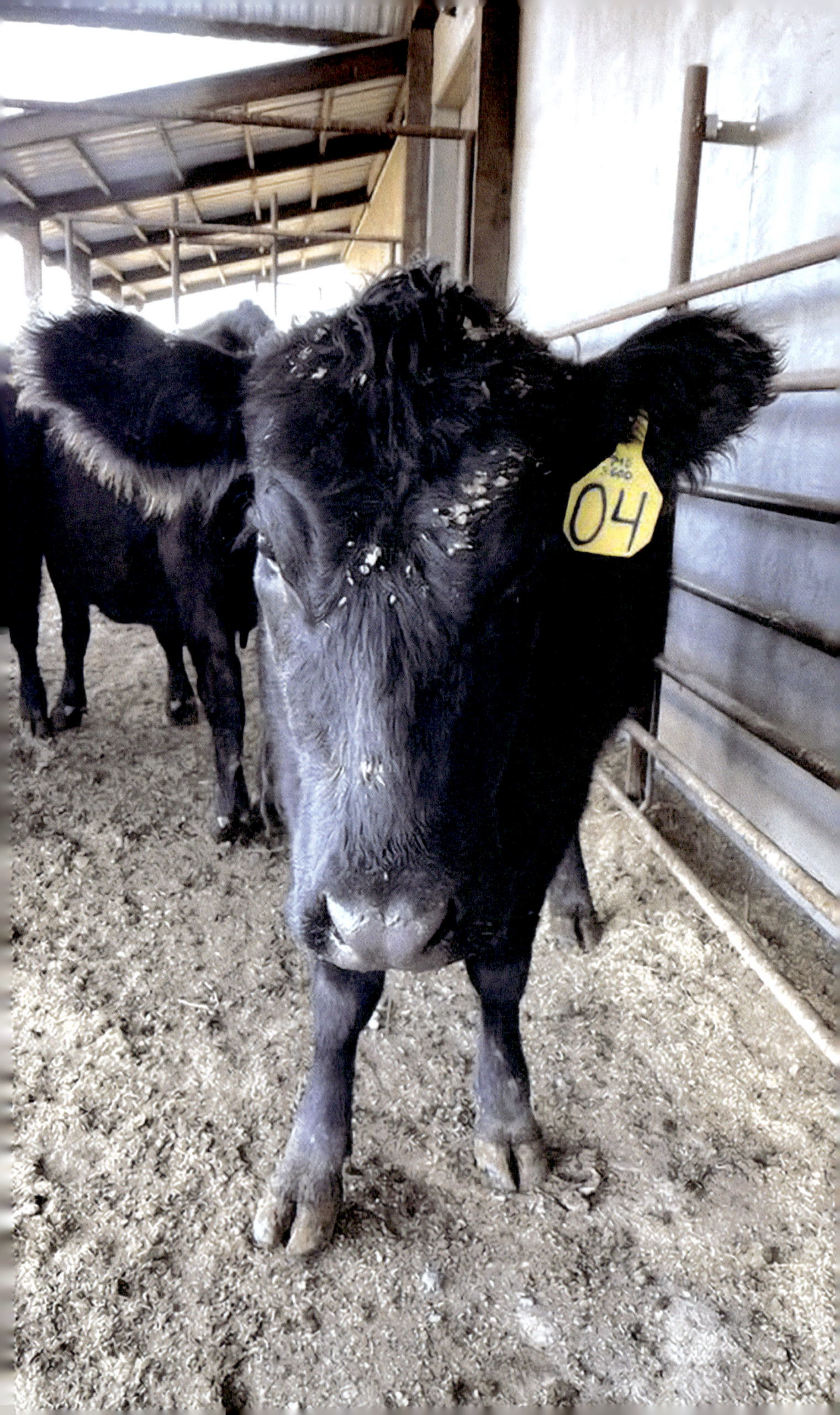
04

She marched into The Sam's with a list and a dream. She needed the huge cases of water that, all wrapped in plastic, resemble a lumpy, fluffy gal in Spanx.

She hoisted the first one into the cart with a thud. Then the second. On the third, her grip loosened in mid-hoist. She hit the cart with the bale of bottles. The cart rolled and she took a step. She hit it again. If she were more athletic, maybe things would have played out differently.

With flashes of middle school basketball embarrassment replaying in her mind, she heaved the water toward the rolling cart and tipped the rim again. The cart was hurtling toward the plastic cutlery at an impressive clip and as she mumbled an epithet toward the biscuit-eating Baptist holy roller cart, it crashed into something solid and she shoved the water over the edge and into the cart.

The woman holding the other cart tsk-tsked her. Ida was sure the woman was adding her to the church prayer list in an attempt to right her heathen ways and she wasn't wrong. The woman said something about *bless her heart* and before she could beat Ida to the punch, Ida told her she would be praying for her.

Bless her heart, indeed.

PHOTO BY LOY COTTEN

THIS IS *Lorabeth*

Her husband scratched his head.

"What are the odds?" he said.

"It will be fine," he said.

They should have bought a lottery ticket instead that night because the odds were better they'd win that, than end up with four babies. But here she is. Alone. Bewildered. Struggling to understand, and well...stand.

Four babies. Four little bundles of joy. Kind of like a double-double-double negative, she can never figure out if it's a negative or positive. Maybe if she could sleep she could figure it out. But the sleeping days have vanished, much like her feet seem to have.

So. Much. Milk. But still not enough. So there are bottles too.

She'll make it through. They'll all survive. Her everything will never be the same, but she's got four darling babies out of it.

But next time a man says, *"What are the odds?"* she's blocking him and buying a lottery ticket.

THANK YOU, MARIA TIBBETTS

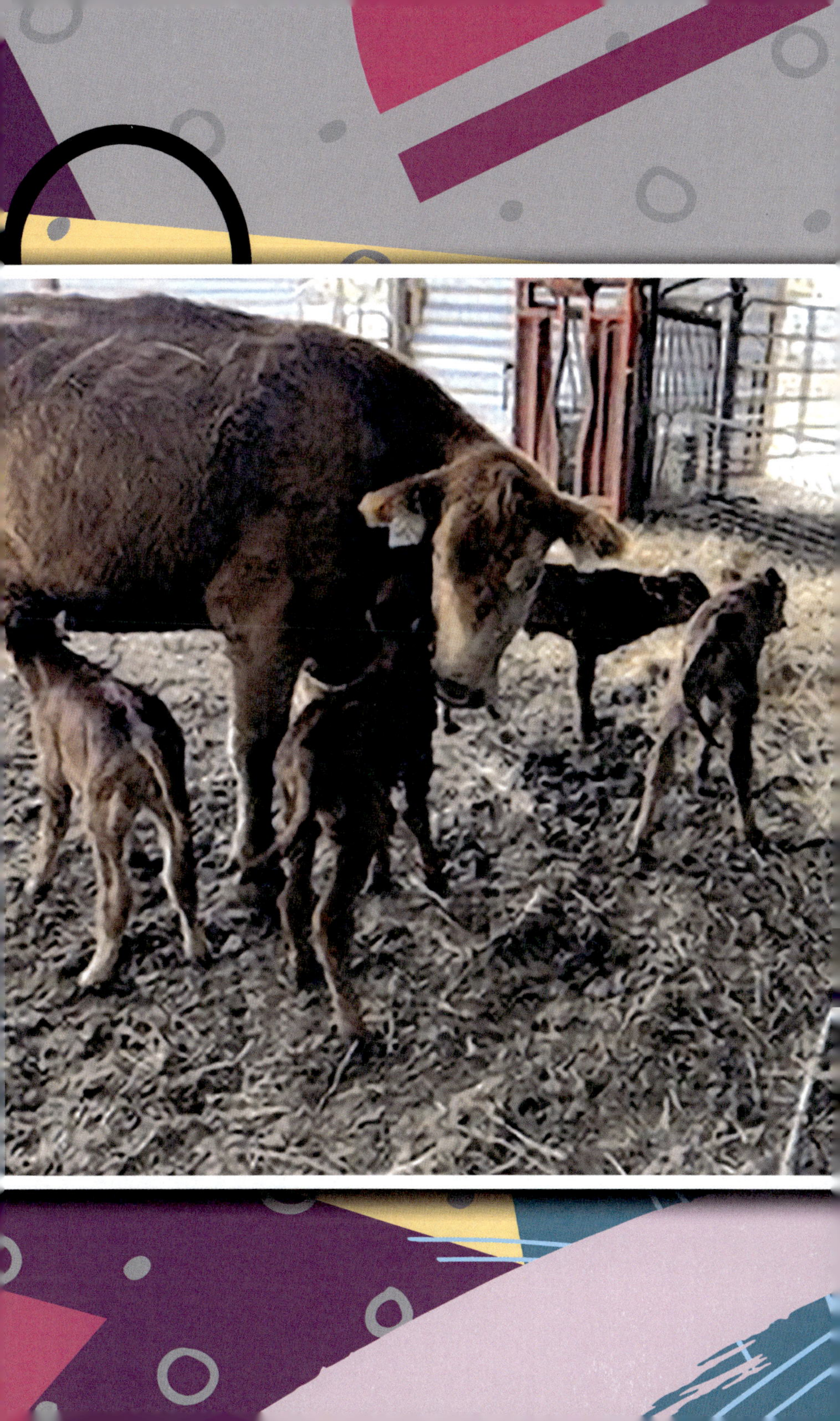

It's Monday, and things are about to get real. Yesterday she celebrated with ham, potatoes, carrot cake, more potatoes, and more carrot cake. This morning she feels like a busted tube of biscuits and has pledged to stick to protein shakes all week.

Every time she walks by the fridge she can hear the carrot cake calling her name. She hears the siren song of the string cheese and sees the come-hither glances of the leftover taters.

Ugh. She doesn't even wish she had the metabolism of a teenager...she just hopes for a metabolism.

~~THIS~~ IS

She is genuinely happy. She has been walking at lunch every day and the endorphins are for reals. She has a happy playlist to listen to and she started keeping a gratitude journal. And she bought new pens for it, obviously.

Today she is thankful for Diet Cherry Limeades. She will cut you if you take a drink of…no, no…what she meant was you're welcome to some. *You want the cherry? Are you freaking kidding?!* What she means is she likes cherries, too.

Oh? She loves girls' get togethers… she would love to hear about your direct sales. Really. Really?

Who is she kidding. Back away from the drink and step back so she can roll her car window up. *With you on the other side.*

Run along. She's reached her limit.

569
3320
8320

F
219
272

THIS IS *Marguerite*

She can remember the lyrics to an impressive number of '80s and '90s country songs, her childhood phone number, that time she tried to do the running man at a school dance, and the song about how a bill comes a law.

She cannot, however, remember what she walked into a room for, what is on her to-do list, and that one thing her husband told her to do just a few hours ago. She thinks her memory might be drunk.

Light a candle for her, girls, but don't expect her to remember to blow it out when she leaves.

Things this winter have been a little hairy. She supposes spring is on its way, and with it, cuffed jeans, capris, and shorts. She's feeling weak at the mere prospect.

Winter leg shaving is not at the top of her priority list but she decided today was the day. A new razor, two head rushes of blood to her brain, and half a can of shaving cream later, the water is still trying to drain and she feels oddly lighter. And colder.

She's still whiter than a fish belly, but slightly more presentable. *Slightly.*

Carry on.

GWS
255

The plan—and there was one—was merely to have a few beers and a burrito. They ran into Coach, and all four of them were slapping each other on the back and guffawing. They talked football, conservative politics, the price of diesel.

One of them suggested they go out to their old hangout. They told stories, drank cheap beer, and laughed.

It all happened quickly, and honestly, he couldn't remember the details. When his wife arrived with the requested tools, she couldn't look at him without seeing his 19-year-old self.

It took a hot minute to free him and he stood, looking sheepishly at his bride who was still holding a pair of bolt cutters. She asked what happened.

He didn't want to tell her so he winked at her and said, *"Safety third, babe. That's us."*

Don't tell OSHAA, ok?

PHOTO BY KATIE CORNELIUS

She was enjoying the spring afternoon with her teenage daughters when they said, *"It's the golden hour, mom. Take a selfie!"* After many failed attempts, she gave up and asked them to take it. They happily obliged.

Upon seeing the result, she objected of the face in the photo. *"Ewww, I don't have any make-up on! No concealer, you can see all of my freckles, age spots, and imperfections!"*

Her daughters promptly replied with the same thing she had told them their entire lives. *"Oh Mama, you're beautiful just the way God made you."*

It was at this moment that her heart melted, all her worries faded away, and she silently thanked God for amazing daughters and the real golden hours.

PHOTO AND BIO BY SALLY HOLDREN

She had been planning lunch with The Besties for weeks and had the best of intentions to stay on the calorie-counting, water-drinking wagon. They were talking and laughing, and pretty soon, she was three margaritas deep and the empty chip baskets were adding up faster than the total in an online shopping cart.

Her friends were no help. They were living their best lives with extra sour cream and flirting with the waiter. Three hours later, they were giggling and weaving out the door and trying to sober up before school pickup.

Thank goodness for pals. And salsa.

PHOTO BY STACY MCCLINTOCK

THIS IS *Georgia*

She just dropped her frequent filler card between her car seat and certain doom. And the dang thing was complete and ready to be redeemed for an expensive and mostly unnecessary beverage of her choosing.

The black hole had been a burial at sea for change, three shades of Mary Kay lippies, several good pens, and a few pens that were just free. It was entirely possible that there was also foreign currency, whole donuts, and a string quartet.

If only she could also lose, in addition to things of value, that nagging feeling that she forgot something, those 15 extra pounds she found, and the need to complete the ranch books.

But, here we are.

KK
9814
214

She made a groundbreaking discovery that she's certain no one else ever has. In fact, she thinks this makes her not only a Pinterest trendsetter, but basically a fit and fab influencer.

She filled her ridiculously large tumbler with ice, cold coffee, and a protein shake. Now, she is caffeinated courtesy of 160 calories rather than her usual 6,239.

About three tumblers deep, she googled it and while she may not be the inventor of the *"profee"* or *"coftein"* or *"replacement for over priced fattening drive thru iced coffee,"* she's had enough now that she's just excited to spread the joyous news.

She's spreading it very quickly, in fact. Her hands are shaking enough that the ice in the tumbler sounds like a Moroccan bride doing the Macarena. She could probably thread a sewing machine while it was running.

She can smell colors, man. If you need her she'll be posting brilliant drink ideas on The Pinterest.

Pass the coffee, man.

She is overtired, overstimulated, overdrafted, and over this week. Yes, she knows she'll miss this stage, but she also knows she's tired.

In her doom scrolling, it appears that all her friends bask in the glow of motherhood, spreading patience and organic snacks like glitter. It appears they don't open the fridge to make dinner and burst into tears, and it appears they understand fifth grade fractions homework.

Meanwhile, she's out here in the wild with snot in her hair, one girl child eye roll away from the devil.

So, she sits in her car for an extra five minutes when she gets home, gathers herself, googles ground beef recipes, and goes inside to win this night.

Light a candle for her, girls.

KC
50
3-1-

While the list isn't comprehensive, she would like to offer you a list of things she would rather do than whatever it is she is procrastinating in order to avoid.

She would rather separate glitter by shape and color. She would rather give up sour cream. She would rather return to bag phones and tight pants. She would rather trade in her iPhone for a Dell with only a floppy disk of *Where in the World is Carmen Sandiego?*

She would rather eat shellfish in rural North Dakota. She would rather jump rope. And, she would rather replay a highlight reel of every time in the past decade she has been weird, awkward, or embarrassed.

Light a candle for her, girls.

THIS IS Mary Jo

She ran errands today with a surprising amount of efficiency, even with her children in tow. She remembered toothpaste, Ziploc bags, and to drop the bag of outgrown clothes at the Goodwill before they became a permanent resident of her car. She checked all the boxes and was putting away groceries, still proud of her mad organizational skills.

Because she's not an actual Olympian who wants to run marathons, she was loading her arms with items to go to the pantry to do it all in one trip. Can of pineapple chunks, pasta sauce, can of green chiles, can of black beans, lemonade mix, and finally, a can of chickpeas.

That's when it happened.

The green chiles rolled into the black beans, and the result was pinching. Not a mild pinch. It was the kind of pinch that reminds some women simultaneously that they ain't 23 anymore, they need to buy a new bra, and things may not actually be looking up.

In an effort to ease the pain and avoid a black bean can-sized nipple piercing, she rolled her armload, dropping the pineapple on her bare foot. It was then, gentle readers, that she let loose a string of expletives that would make Jelly Roll blush and Kid Rock divert his eyes.

The swelling is markedly more noticeable on one side now, and the developing bruise smacks of questionable behavior and a midlife crisis more than an unfortunate run-in with tropical fruit and high-protein side dishes.

What's better? Heading to town in the morning for a two-fer—her annual mammogram and once-over at the dermatologist, scheduled in a fit of efficiency, obviously.

If you need her, she'll be spending the day explaining that she is, in fact, safe at home and no, it really was just a grocery mishap and not the result of anything weird.

Bless her heart.

816
216

825

February is dumb for a couple of reasons, the least of which is the entire world's inability to pronounce it without sounding like Hooked on Phonics, did indeed, work for them. It is also often muddy, often cold, and often warm enough to lull the naive and hopeful into believing spring is right around the corner.

That is, until you enter the door of a north-facing building and have to walk like an old woman just looking for someone to thump with her purse.

The cherry on top, though, is the pre-April bookwork. Some people found the $3.41 that kept their accounts from balancing. Some people found their password after not logging into their accounting program since last April. They are not the same.

Pray for them all, girls. But mostly their long suffering accountants.

THIS IS Shania

She was doom scrolling after 2 a.m. and wondering why exactly all the hip young people were wearing flat sunglasses. She thought they resembled something between a bug guard on a 1987 Ford pickup and a welding helmet.

Goodness knows when she was 20-something, she was wearing completely reasonable, classic pieces. Keyhole blouses with Aztec print, a cape, and cropped to sit well above her below-boob-level Rockies worn stacked to her knees were basically timeless. Then there were striped jeans that revealed, to those you walked away from, a star on your backside of darker denim.

And lest we forget pony bead and concho boot bracelets on pearly white Ropers or polyester braided belts or even polyester jackets that made more noise than a toddler with a fruit roll up wrapper.

Yep, she thinks, *thank goodness we didn't bow to dumb trends.*

Pass the White Rain, girls.

ICON
891
291

THIS IS *LaDonna*

In her defense, she would have been more forthcoming had the young newbie officer given her a chance to explain. He saw her Suburban speeding down the county road. It wasn't even 8 a.m. when he radioed dispatch. He couldn't see into her back windows through the thick coat of dirt road, and he rested his hand on his weapon as he approached the vehicle.

She was trying to conceal a smile and explain her morning thus far when he asked exactly what it was she found so entertaining about reckless driving. It went downhill from there. There were radio conversations and while he couldn't see anyone else in the vehicle, he felt certain he had seen a figure in the very back. He was sure he heard a thump. There was no telling what she might be hiding. He had seen all of the *Chicago PD* episodes and he knew it was always the ones you didn't suspect.

He marched her to the back of her vehicle about the time the sheriff pulled up. The sheriff had known her since she was a kid and was about to ask why the young buck had her out of the vehicle. He asked her curtly to open the back door and when she did, he drew his weapon before the sheriff could stop what was about to unfold.

Two wet baby calves, warm now after riding under the car heater to school drop-off and halfway back home, lurched toward him with a bawl. One wobbled and tipped into his chest, smearing him with slime and black tar calf poop and violating his shades with a wet tongue.

The old sheriff considered tossing the young buck a rag but decided against it, told LaDonna she was free to go, and told her to tell her family hello.

And that was the last time the newbie pulled her over during calving season.

Valentines

I'm stuck on you like an Eat Beef sticker on a bale bed.

You brighten my day like a Golight during calving season.

We click like a well-oiled calf puller.

You're the calving ease bull to my first calf heifer.

My love for you is more bountiful than an armload of uterine prolapse and longer lasting than a shoelace stitch job.

I'm stuck on you like a Muck boot on a bare foot.

You make my heart race like a limit up report on sale day.

You spin the crank to the head gate of my heart.

I love you more than a farm dog loves bull-calf castration day.

You're hotter than the defroster on a clean dashboard in March.

I'm happier to see you than a farm dog on a flatbed turning into the neighbor's.

PHOTO BY TRACY MOORE

THIS IS *Genevieve*

When evaluating her goals for the new year, she wants to improve her figure. She's not talking about the 38/36/40 but the 17,207/72/166.

There are people with clean inboxes, clean missed call logs, and read text messages, but she's not on that list.

She wants to improve her record against the chicken that gets out, hides in a tumbleweed, and then flaps at her head like possessed shrapnel, leaving her cursing and bleeding.

She wants to improve her record of days she doesn't spill coffee on herself. She wants to improve the average time wet clothes sit in the washer before remembering them and moving them to the dryer, narrowly escaping mildew.

She wants to improve her record against goat head stickers. *Isn't that what everyone wants?*

It doesn't seem oddly specific to her, it's fine. Everything's *fine.*

PHOTO BY ANN LITTLE

THIS IS *Ginny*

She had been waiting for a particular package to come in the mail and her email said it had arrived. Granted, the post office tends to start with *"what package?"* and end with *"it has been delivered. It appears your porch light bulb is burned out and you forgot to plug in your slow cooker. Here is an alternative recipe for tater tot casserole that will use the pound of ground in your fridge."*

The box was lying opened and empty. The coffee pot was empty and so was the chocolate stash. She heard a strange snorting noise coming from the good chair in what should have been an empty house. She crept closer, following the little foil chocolate wrapper trail.

When she heard the snorting noise again, she followed it and found the book and the source of the snorting and empty chocolate wrappers. Her husband had come back early and was wiping tears from his eyes and holding her book.

"I thought you said I wouldn't like these...I recognize a number of the cows in my life in here."

A lesser woman may have been offended but, she, too, recognized many of the cows, including herself, in the book. Who said #cowbios are just for The Girls?

She has seen the light. She was flying—er, driving—down the gravel road (yes, at a reasonable and cautious speed, being aware of washboards and wildlife) when she saw it. She could see the glow for miles - she does live in the flat country, but still—it was miles and miles.

The glow continued to approach, eclipsing the moon and the one visible yard light. She crested the one hill in her county and it happened. Her retinas were seared and smoldering, and tears came to her eyes. She grabbed the wheel, hit the brakes, tried not to drive into the sandy abyss of the bar ditch where she may never been seen again.

She turned the radio completely off and dropped her phone. She was sure the world was on fire. The writing on her tee shirt, her eye color, and the dark circles under her eyes were surely all visible from space.

And then, after what seemed like a lifetime, it was gone and she plunged back into darkness. She looked in her rearview mirror with the limited sight that remained to see the vehicle's driver flip their high beams on.

Sweet baby Jesus, the headlights get brighter?!

She tried to rub her eyes to rid them of the unicorns and dancing cupcakes in her line of vision and hoped that was the only car she would pass tonight.

Light a candle for her, girls, but not one with an LED light.

THIS IS

She is headed to find an outfit that will work for a holiday party or two. She passed on the one-piece jumpsuit for obvious reasons. She also passed on a variety of slinky, minky, sequined, and based on a bag of Jiffy Pop-type get-ups. She was beginning to think there were no clothes for the middle ground between Shakira and Margaret Thatcher.

About the time she was resigning herself to wearing sweats, she spotted them. Faux leather leggings with belly-smoothing, butt-lifting, fortune-telling, recyclable, sustainable, vegan, and jiggle-supporting abilities.

When it was time to party, she shimmied and shook and smeared into those babies, paired them with her favorite fancy denim shirt, and walked into the kitchen, triumphant. Her husband, who fancies himself a comedian, bent down and fixed his hair in the reflection of her thigh.

Without missing a beat, she snatched his hat off his head and fixed her lipstick in the reflection that was revealed.

And this is marriage, folks.

PHOTO BY LOY COTTON

04

153
190

THESE ARE *The Aunties*

Here today with a bit of Thanksgiving advice for a day of less bitchin' and more kitchen. Take the rolls out of the freezer first thing before you forget. Say a quick prayer to the patron saint of Pam spray and give thanks to the inventor of aluminum foil.

If there were ever a day to use fancy coffee creamer and a squirt of whipped topping, baby, it's today. If your veggie tray looks more like a storm on radar than a turkey, don't sweat it. Use powdered sugar in heavy whipping cream and you'll change someone's life.

If you haven't mopped yet, it's fine. No one will notice, and if they do, it's because they are intimately familiar with the look of an unmopped floor. Take the time to force your guests to tell what they're thankful for before the meal - you can learn a lot from a hungry person under pressure.

Enjoy the day. It's fine, everything is *fine*. One of The Aunties once spilled turkey grease on her hot oven and floor, slipped in the grease, fell, and blew out her knee. Before you lay there in poultry grease on your unmopped floor, just remember you're doing fine.

So what if the fire alarm summons everyone to the table? *We won't tell*. But seriously, take the rolls out so they can rise.

THIS IS *Marti*

She's slightly hungover from the thermos she and her mom pals took with them trick-or-treating last night. She ate enough Reese's that she has peanut butter in her blood stream and has already had enough coffee this morning that she could thread a sewing machine while it's running.

She finally drug her children out the door to go to school, started the 'Burb, and Christmas music began blaring from the speakers. Two things appear to be true: with the radio cranked this loud from last night, she was clearly a different person back then. Secondly, the Food Channel programming is about to get butter-soaked, frosted, sprinkled, toasted, and cheers-ed.

She's here for it, man. *She's here for it.*

THIS IS *Maggie*

Her daughter who, yesterday, was too mature and sophisticated to dress up for Halloween, decided *this morning* to wear a costume. She nearly spit coffee out her nose when she told Maggie she would be dressing up as, well, Maggie.

Her dear teen daughter told her she couldn't decide which version to choose. The messy bun Maggie, with tummy control leggings, a bucket of cleaning supplies, and a murder podcast? The ranch Maggie, complete with multiple layers of clothes, mismatched gloves, and a sorting stick? The office day Maggie, with a laptop, a migraine, and five coffee cups? Or perhaps the town trip Maggie, with a box of parts from John Deere, a pile of reusable grocery bags, boxes of beer, a nearly empty large Sonic cup, and *another* huge tumbler?

Sweet daughter giggled and said Maggie would just have to wait until the school costume parade to find out. Pray for her, girls. Pray for her.

THIS IS Mirabel

She loaded the kids and rolled out to the pumpkin patch so they could have a fun day—and maybe she could even snap a great photo to use on her Christmas cards.

After paying exorbitant ticket prices, they took in the sights. They went to the slide first. She watched her kids and a few other moms fit on the burlap sacks and swoosh down the slide.

After realizing how much of her cheeks would hang over each side of the burlap, remembering just how hot October can still be on a metal slide, and hearing her sweaty thighs making noises similar to a 1987 Subaru with a manual transmission and a driver who needs an automatic, she scooted and smeared to the bottom.

Oh, yes. She was having fun now.

Her kids filled a wagon with pumpkins, gourds, and the variety of heirloom squash found in the fancy magazines and she hoped her debit card wouldn't decide to shut off to avoid "fraudulent charges" in the hundreds of dollars.

Finally, after a spin through the corn maze with someone else's booger-covered child rather than her own, they took a sweaty and sunburned selfie and called it a day.

She had nearly forgotten the lower moments of the day until she spent a few quality hours vacuuming corn kernels out of her car, washer, dryer, shoes, floor, kids' beds...

It's okay, Mirabel. Those burlap sacks are *really* narrow. That's our story, and we're sticking to it.

She doesn't know the question, but she knows the answer is shredded cheese.

Rough day? Kids fighting, dog came untrained, no idea what to make for dinner? Start with shredded cheese.

Husband grumpy, jury duty notification in the mailbox, and no clean underwear? Shredded cheese.

Look like you have it all together, but in reality, your socks keep coming off your heel, your car needs fuel, and it's really windy? Shredded cheese.

Cheers to a girl with the answers.

THIS IS *Jenna*

She has a million-dollar idea that will save marriages—and might save a life.

For a small monthly subscription fee—less than a cup of coffee a day—she will provide men with a number to video call. Female operators will be standing by. The male caller can tell the operator what he's looking for—ketchup, for example—and the operator will tell him where it is.

This avoids the temptation of said man to ask his wife and then stand in front of the open fridge looking for something that is *right in front of him.* It will save energy, too. Very climate conscious.

She's going to make bank. You can call her girl boss.

PHOTO BY LOY COTTEN

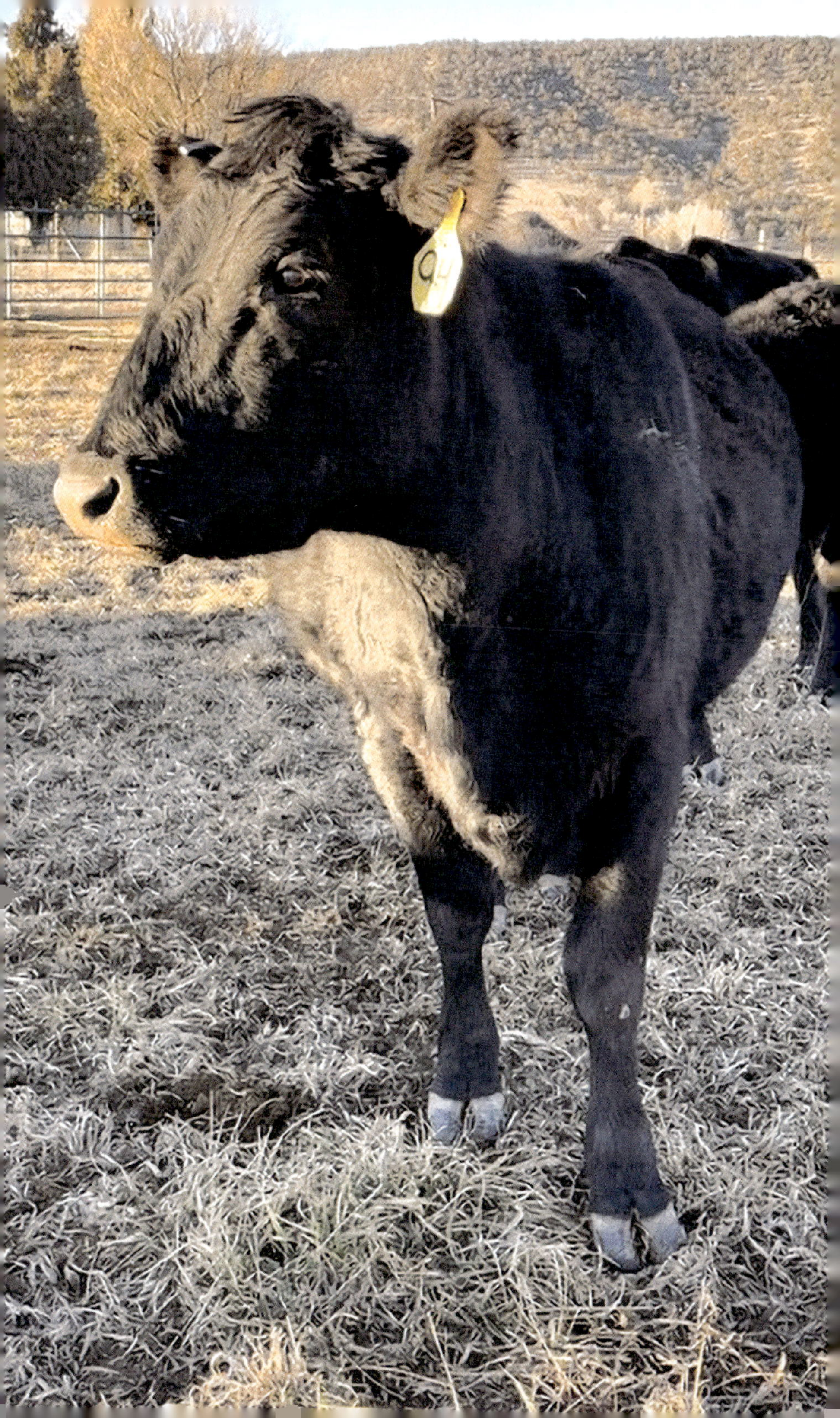

THIS IS *Hannah*

She has decided to try meal planning so her family will quit teasing her about her spaghetti–taco–burger–roast rotation. She turned on *The Pioneer Woman* show and got to work. The recipes weren't anything weird—no fish, nothing that can't be found at the small town Safeway. She wasn't watching Ina Garten, after all.

The first new recipe garnered praise like, "what is this? Where are the tacos?"

The second night a kid asked who she was and what she had done with his mom.

The third night a kid said she went all day not knowing what day it was because she hadn't eaten tacos the night before.

The next week, she returned to *The Rotation.*

Glory be, man.

THIS IS *June*

Despite the videos she has studied, it appears that perhaps contouring and highlighting makeup tutorials are, in fact, *not* as easy as the well-blended crowd may hope to convey. She thought she nailed it—until she caught a look at herself in broad daylight.

Luckily, June knows a few things to be true: beauty isn't for the faint of heart, she read enough beauty quizzes in *Teen Magazine* circa 1990-something to know things are on a positive trajectory, and it takes a lot of money to look cheap.

Keep it real, June. Keep it real.

June
5
06

THIS IS *Vanna*

She and her kids listen to trivia-for-kids podcasts because they're cool cats. Today, she couldn't answer a single question in the spooky movie category. She hadn't even heard of the shows referenced in the Disney Channel category, but the '90s category? *Shut the front door, kids*. She spouted answers like a woman possessed:

Hey, Macarena!

Tickle Me, Elmo!

Pop Rocks Candy!

Friends!

Book It!

A mall!

A pager!

Did her children gaze at her with adoration and respect in their teary eyes? Did her children applaud her knowledge? Did her children beg for more wisdom to be imparted upon their young minds?

No. No, they didn't. They still think she made up the pager—a little rectangular thing that people would call and punch a number into for you to find a landline phone with which to return their numerical, character-only message.

Fun haters.

PHOTO BY LOY COTTON

She hooked the little flatbed trailer to her SUV and headed out to pick up straw bales for the fall decor-a-palooza happening in her yard.

She rolled into the farm store, and the kid pointed to the pile and asked her if she could back her trailer to it.

"You bet."

"Are you sure? I can back it for you if you want," he smiled at her like the guy at the mechanic shop does when he bends down and speaks clearly and slowly to her about complicated topics like oil weights and tire pressure.

She smiled at him and said she would back it herself. Feeling pressure similar to the contestants in the final round of *Miss America, Ultimate Cowboy,* and *The Voice*, she pulled forward and saw the growing crowd of high school boys watching her.

She pulled forward, navigated around another pickup, around a stray cart, around three stacks of shavings, cut it hard right, and backed up squarely to the pile. Proof positive that the good Lord looks out for babies, fools, and the occasional trailer-driving mama.

She needs to jump on her banking app to make sure she, you know, has money.

Incorrect password.

She went through the reset process and entered a password.

New password must be different than previous ten attempts.

Lila has two passwords, friends. She flip-flops between them, but apparently the banking app has proven to be a formidable foe.

Lilalou1977$

Nope.

Iheartcows77

Nope.

RockyMtnjeans78;

Nope.

Thisisstupid911$

Nope.

Forshitssake77)

Nope.

Aaaahhh356!

Success! Go to login page.

Invalid password.

Mothertrucker77&

Success! Go to login page.

Invalid password.

Invalid password.

If only there were a way to just look at the checkbook and know the balance. Someone should really look into that, she thought, because this girl is out of passwords.

THIS IS *Fanny*

She has spent far too many hours alone this week.

She hauled a few loads of corn to the elevator where, while in the dump-line, she masterfully won a fake argument with the lady that cut in line at the Safeway three days ago.

She sat patiently in the school parking lot long enough to remaster the ageless "Shoop" by Salt 'n Pepa.

Last night, she munched on saltines in the kitchen, watching reels about bathroom cleaning hacks long after the rest of the house was tucked in bed because she couldn't resist that fourth iced coffee at 5 p.m.

And then, to everyone's horror and amazement, she learned the latest TikTok dance while the stock tank filled at the pasture. And by "everyone," she means the school bus carrying her children and the rest of the rural-route kids.

Light a candle girls, she's got some 'splainin to do! Shoop!

THANK YOU, NIKI WERNSMAN. PHOTO BY LOY COTTEN

H

This morning, she woke up extra early to ensure she had time to grab a shower and some mascara because this week, she's not exactly winning.

On Monday, she was late running kids to school, so she mumbled a prayer to the patron saint of holy leggings and Muck boots, and ran out the door looking 87% homeless. It was the morning she was summoned by the PTA Moms who were gathered with their fresh extensions and Uggs to discuss after-holiday concert snacks. She didn't expect to get out of the car.

The next day, the shirt and leggings she wanted were in the dryer and she was in a hurry to get outside to help sort calves. As she streaked through the kitchen en route to the dryer, she looked up to see the brand inspector and the neighbor sitting—and looking stunned—at the table. She hit the ground like a cowboy in a spaghetti Western shot off his steed and crawled back to the bedroom.

Today, though, she's determined that no employees of the state will be forced to grapple with any unintentional visuals of her stomach and thighs. She's determined that if summoned out of her vehicle, she'll be able to do so without bystanders wondering where she parked her stolen grocery cart. She probably won't see another soul all day.

Light a candle for the brand inspector and the neighbor guy, man.

About the Author

Rachel Gabel is a longtime agriculture writer and farm broadcaster and she writes and reports from her family's cow calf operation in northeastern Colorado. She is the assistant editor of *The Fence Post Magazine*, on-air on *Western Ag Network*, and pens a weekly ag and rural issues column that appears in *Colorado Politics, Denver Gazette*, and *Colorado Springs Gazette*.

Gabel has written six children's books, five of which have been used in classrooms by Colorado Agriculture in the Classroom and Logan County Cattlewomen's Association to bring agriculture to kids.

She began writing #cowbios in a goat barn in December of 2022. She took a quite glamorous photo of a goat with an underbite. She called her Linda. Linda was a divorcee and a good bowler and knew her prince would arrive in a less-than-practical car and custom bowling shoes. She made a mean pina colada and is contemplating teeth whitening like the gal at the post office.

Gabel has posted every weekday ever since.

The community that has developed crisscrosses the country to make fun of themselves and trade 90s references. They're absolutely the best kinds of weirdos.

Rachel's books are available at Rachelgabel.com and at the occasional feed store, veterinary office, livestock market, and hardware store.

Cattle, Corn, and Courage:
The Story of Dr. John Matsushima

Kindergarten Cowman

Light a Candle for Her, Girls

The Woolly Way:
Papou and the Story of Lantern Ridge

The Sweetest Treat

Still Good: The Faces of Family Agriculture

Kindergarten Rancher

Available at www.RachelGabel.com

Acknowledgments

I get by with a little help from my friends.

Thank you for the ideas, photos, and occasional #cowbio. The photos you take covertly at the State Fair and The Walmart are gold, too. Keep those coming.

And for Liz Munsterteiger, the sole reason my books are spectacularly beautiful. I'm proud to work with you.

Made in the USA
Middletown, DE
09 December 2024